Greedylocks

Written by
Alan Durant

Illustrated by
Rory Walker

Greedylocks was a girl with a big appetite.

Here she is eating her breakfast: bacon, eggs, sausages, ham, toast, jam, blueberry muffins and three bowls of sugary cornflakes – all washed down with two banana milkshakes and a giant mug of hot chocolate.

Here she is eating her lunch.

Here she is eating her tea.

Here she is eating her dinner.

Here she is eating her late-night snack.

Meanwhile in an apartment nearby, on the edge of the wood, there lived a baby bear who would not eat his food.

One morning, Mummy Bear served out the porridge for breakfast: a large bowlful for Daddy Bear, a medium-sized bowlful for Mummy Bear and a small bowlful for Baby Bear.

Daddy Bear added a swirl of skimmed milk to his porridge. Mummy Bear added a sprinkle of salt to her porridge. Baby Bear added a teaspoon of honey to **his** porridge.

But he didn't eat it. He made it into a volcano.

"Let's go for a jog while we wait for the porridge to cool down," said Mummy Bear.

"Good idea," said Daddy Bear. "That will give Baby Bear an appetite."

"Humph!" said Baby Bear.

Meanwhile Greedylocks was riding her scooter through the wood to get some more food from the shops, when she smelt something rather nice …

She walked into the bears' kitchen and licked her greedy lips.

First she sat on Daddy Bear's chair and tasted his porridge. But the chair was too low and the porridge too healthy.

Mummy Bear's chair was too low too, and her porridge was too salty.

"Yuk!" said Greedylocks.

But Baby Bear's chair was just right and his porridge was delicious.

"Yum," she said – and she ate it all up.

Meanwhile Daddy Bear had climbed a tree and was picking apples.

He passed them down to Mummy Bear.

She offered one to Baby Bear.

Baby Bear took the apple ... and kicked it into the air.

Meanwhile Greedylocks sighed contentedly, leant back on Baby Bear's chair and – CRACK, CRASH! – it broke and she fell on her big bottom.

Meanwhile Baby Bear was on Daddy Bear's shoulders, as he and Mummy Bear walked home.

Meanwhile Greedylocks had eaten everything in the bears' fridge and was feeling rather sleepy. So she went upstairs to find a bed to rest on.

First, she lay down on Daddy Bear's bed
"Too hard," she said.

Then she lay down on Mummy Bear's bed.
"Too crowded," she said.

But Baby Bear's bed was just right. "This is so cosy," she said – and she snuggled right in and turned on the TV.

Meanwhile Daddy Bear, Mummy Bear and Baby Bear arrived back at their cottage.

"Someone's been sitting on my chair and tasting my porridge," said Daddy Bear.

"Someone's been sitting on my chair and tasting my porridge," said Mummy Bear.

"Someone's been sitting on my chair and they've broken it!" cried Baby Bear. "And they've eaten all my porridge!"

"And they've emptied our fridge!" said Mummy Bear.

Meanwhile upstairs, Greedylocks started to snore.

Downstairs, Daddy Bear said, "What's that terrible noise?"

The three bears went upstairs to see.

"Someone's been lying on my couch," said Daddy Bear.

"Someone's been lying on my bed," said Mummy Bear. "and they've disturbed my teddies."

"Quick, come and see!" squeaked Baby Bear. "Someone's lying in my bed right now!"

At that moment Greedylocks woke up.

She saw the three bears looking down at her, as if they were going to eat her.

"Yikes!" she yelled and she leapt out of bed, raced down the stairs and out of the house. She jumped on her scooter and scooted as fast as she could.

"Yippee!" shouted Baby Bear as he chased her home.

Baby Bear skipped back happily. "That was so much fun!" he said. "I'm hungry."

"That greedy girl stole all our food," said Mummy Bear.

"We have some lovely apples," said Daddy Bear.

Baby Bear ate one, two, three apples.

"Delicious," he said. "Can I have one more?"

Meanwhile Greedylocks took out the food she'd stolen from the bears' fridge and grinned greedily. Those bears thought they would eat her; well, she was going to have the last laugh!

But somebody else wanted his breakfast too! And he didn't want to eat bears' food.

His breakfast had long golden hair!